ISBN 1 85854 1441
© Brimax Books Ltd, 1988.
This edition published by Brimax Books Ltd,
Newmarket, England, 1994.
Reprinted 1995.
Printed in France - n° 64243

THE FORGETFUL
SPIDER

By
June Woodman

Illustrated by
Ken Morton

Brimax . Newmarket . England

6

The Forgetful Spider

Spider is putting on his shoes.
He is going to Kangaroo's
party. He counts his shoes
as he puts them on.
"One, two, three, four, five,
six, seven . . ." Only seven
shoes for EIGHT feet!
"Oh dear, I have lost one
of my shoes," says Spider.
He looks in his house but he
cannot find the shoe anywhere.

He goes to look for the shoe.
He meets Elephant. Elephant
is busy picking oranges.
"Hello, Elephant. Have you seen
my shoe?" asks Spider.
"No," says Elephant, "and I am
far too busy to look for it.
If you see Alligator, tell
him I will bring oranges
to Kangaroo's party."
"I shall probably forget,"
says Spider.

Spider sets off to look for
Alligator. As he runs along,
one shiny shoe falls off.
Spider does not see it.
Alligator is on the muddy
river bank.
"Hello, Spider," shouts
Alligator. He waves his tail.
SPLOSH! The mud splashes
spider's shiny shoes.

Spider forgets all about
the oranges.
"Look at my shoes!" he cries.
"They are not shiny now."
"Sorry, Spider," says Alligator.
Spider counts his shoes.
"One, two, three, four,
five, six . . ."
"You have lost two shoes,"
says Alligator.
"Have you seen them?"
asks Spider.
"No," says Alligator.

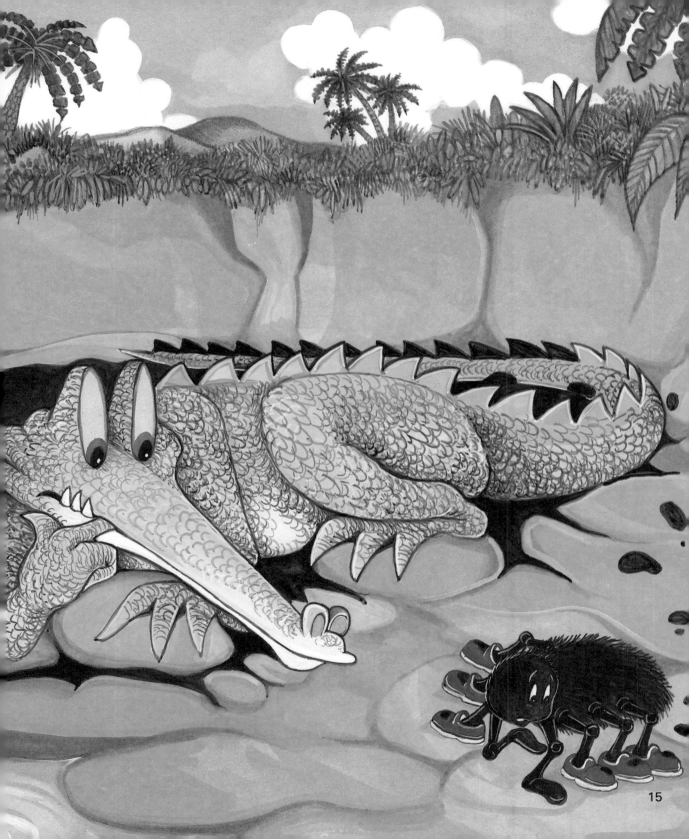

15

"Go and ask Mouse," says
Alligator, "and tell her
I will bring a cake
to Kangaroo's party."
"I shall probably forget,"
says Spider. He sets off
to look for Mouse. As he
runs along, another shoe
falls off. But Spider
does not see it.

Boom! Boom! Boom!
It is Mouse. She is playing
her drum. What a noise!
"Hey Spider!" says Mouse.
"Where are your shoes?"
Spider forgets all about the
cake. He counts his shoes again.
"One, two, three, four, five."
Only five shoes for eight feet.

"I have lost three shoes now,"
says Spider. "Do you know
where they are?"
"No," says Mouse. "Have you
asked Lion? Maybe he can
help. If you see Lion, tell him
I will take my drum
to Kangaroo's party."
"I shall probably forget,"
says Spider.

Spider sets off again.
As he runs, another shoe
falls off. He does not see it.
There is Lion. He is asleep,
as usual, under a tree.
Lion opens one eye.
"Hello, Spider. You have lost
four of your shoes," he says.

Spider forgets about the drum.
"Oh, not another shoe," cries
Spider. He counts his shoes.
"One, two, three, four . . ."
Four shoes for EIGHT feet.
Lion is much too tired
to help Spider look for them.
"Ask Kangaroo," says Lion
with a yawn. "She may know."

"Oh, Spider," says Lion, "tell Kangaroo I will bring flowers to her party."
"I shall probably forget," says Spider. As he runs off, another shoe falls off.
But still he does not see!
He meets Kangaroo.
"Hello, Spider. Where are your shoes?" she cries.

Spider forgets about the flowers.
He counts his shoes.
"One, two, three . . ."
Only three shoes left.
Spider begins to cry.
"Cheer up, Spider," says
Kangaroo. "You are just in time
for my party."
"Party?" sobs Spider. "Oh dear,
I forgot about your party."

Look. Here comes Elephant.
He is carrying some oranges
and one of Spider's shoes.
Along comes Alligator with
a cake and another shoe.
There is Mouse carrying her drum
and another shoe. Lion has
some flowers and another shoe.
Spider begins to count.
"I have three shoes. That makes
four . . . five . . . six . . . seven."

Poor Spider. Still only
seven shoes for eight feet.
But Kangaroo says, "Hey Spider.
Look in my pouch."
There is the lost shoe.
"Remember! You gave it to me
yesterday to clean it,"
says Kangaroo. "Bring me
the other seven tomorrow
and I will clean them too."
"Thank you," says Spider,
"but I shall probably forget."

33

Here are some words in the story.

counts	muddy
lost	another
busy	asleep
party	opens
forget	tired
shiny	yawn
falls	pouch

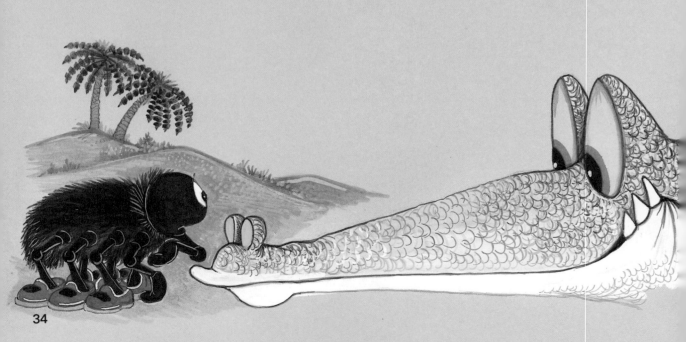

Here are some pictures in the story.

shoes

oranges

cake

drum

flowers

35

The Lazy Lion

It is the Jungle Sports Day.
The sun is hot and the path
is dusty. Lion is looking for
somewhere cool to rest.
"I need a good, long sleep,"
he says.
Soon he comes to the river
and stops for a drink.
Alligator is up a tree.
He is tying flags onto
a long string.

"Hey Lion! Can you help me?"
calls Alligator. Lion yawns.
"Not today. I am much too
tired," he says. "But why
are you tying flags, Alligator?"
he asks.
"Because . . . wo–o–o–o . . ."
Alligator trips over the
flags. SPLAT. He lands
in the mud.
"Never mind," says Lion, and
he goes on down the path.

He sees Kangaroo come bouncing
by with her baby in her pouch.
"Hello, Lion," shouts Kangaroo.
"Are you ready for the big day?"
"Not today, Kangaroo,"
says Lion. "I am much too
tired. What big day?" he asks.
"Sorry, Lion," says Kangaroo.
"Must be going. In training,"
and away she bounces.
"Never mind," says Lion.

Lion wanders on down the dusty path. Elephant is under the trees blowing up balloons.

"All these balloons," he says grumpily. "Will you hold some for me, Lion?"

"Not today," says Lion. "I am much too tired." Lion begins to walk away. He does not see the balloons lift Elephant off the ground.

Lion looks back. "Why are you blowing up balloons, Elephant?" he asks. But Elephant is not there. He is floating away above Lion's head.
"Never mind," says Lion.
He turns and walks on in search of a quiet place to sleep.

Lion sees Spider trying to put
on his running shoes.
"Can you help me tie my shoes?"
asks Spider. "I forget how
to do it."
"Not today, Spider," says Lion.
"I am much too tired. But why
are you wearing running shoes?"
"I forget," says Spider, "but I
know there is a good reason."
"Never mind," says Lion, as he
walks on.

49

Parrot is trying to wind up
his stopwatch.
"Hello, Lion. Hello, Lion,"
says Parrot. "Can you help?
Can you help?"
"Not today. I am much
too tired," says Lion. "But
why are you winding up
a stopwatch?"
"Today is the day, today is
the day . . ." Parrot begins.
"Oh never mind," says Lion.

"That Parrot always says everything twice," says Lion as he gets back to his den. Ostrich is waiting for him. She has Lion's invitation to the sports day. "Hello, Lion," whispers Ostrich, starting to blush. She holds out the invitation.

"Not today, Ostrich," says Lion, "I am much too tired. What is it about, anyway?"

But Ostrich is so shy she puts
her bucket over her head
and she runs away.
"Never mind," says Lion.
He is too lazy to look at
the invitation.
"I think I will get a drink
before I settle down," he says
to himself. He wanders slowly
down to the river. Lion has
a drink and falls asleep.

He does not see that he is
lying on the starting line.
He does not notice the other
animals lining up for the first
race. He does not see Kangaroo
bouncing up and down. Or Spider
with his running shoes on. Or
Hippo on tip-toes. Or Alligator
tripping over his feet and
falling into Ostrich.

He does not see Mouse standing on a box, holding a starting pistol. Or Parrot holding the stopwatch.
Mouse calls out, "Ready, Get Set . . ."
BANG! She fires the starting pistol. Lion wakes up with a start. He jumps to his feet and runs off as fast as he can.

Lion runs past all the other animals. He runs through the finishing tape and keeps going until . . .BUMP! He crashes into Elephant. Elephant has just landed with his balloons. "Out of my way, Elephant!" shouts Lion. "Someone is shooting at me."

All the other animals come
running up to Lion.
"Well done, Lion," they all
shout. "You have won the race."
"In a world record. In a world
record," says Parrot.
"Have a balloon," says Elephant.
"Not today, Elephant," replies
Lion. "I am far too tired.
I must find somewhere
for a quiet sleep."

63

Here are some words in the story.

dusty wearing
stops twice
tying waiting
training blush
bounces lazy
wanders starting
quiet past

Here are some pictures in the story.

flags

balloons

running shoes

stopwatch

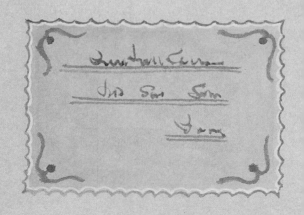

invitation

65

The Clumsy Alligator

Alligator has big feet. He has
a big tail too. Sometimes
he trips over his big feet.
Sometimes he trips over his
big tail. And sometimes he
trips over everything. Then
all his friends laugh. They
call him the clumsy alligator.

One day Alligator is walking
along when he sees Ostrich
picking plums.
"Hello, Ostrich," he shouts.
But Alligator does not see
the log Ostrich is standing on.
He bumps into it. CRASH!
Ostrich tumbles to the ground.
The bucket lands on her head.
"Oops," says Alligator.

Alligator helps take the bucket off Ostrich's head.

"Stay away from me, Alligator," she cries. She gets up and runs off over the stepping stones to the other side of the river.

"Sorry, Ostrich," shouts Alligator.

He turns away and goes to look
for his friend Lion. He sees
him lying in the grass. Lion is
asleep as usual. Alligator
runs up to his friend.
But he does not see his tail.
He steps on it very hard.
"Aaaarr," roars Lion.

"Oops!" says Alligator.
Lion is very cross.
"You clumsy animal," says Lion.
"I am going over the river
to find a quiet place to rest."
Lion goes across the stepping
stones.
"Sorry, Lion," says Alligator.
"Stay away from me," roars Lion.

Alligator heads back to his
muddy bank. His friend Spider
comes to see him.
"Hey Alligator," calls Spider.
"Look at my new shoes!"
Alligator waves his long tail.
Bits of mud go flying through
the air.

Spider starts to run but it is
too late. SPLASH!
Down comes the mud, all over
Spider's new shoes.
"Oops," says Alligator.
"Look at my new shoes,"
moans Spider.
He runs away from Alligator.
He goes across the river on the
stepping stones.

"Sorry, Spider," shouts Alligator.
"Stay away from me," cries
Spider. Alligator decides to go
and see his friend Kangaroo.
She is picking flowers with
her baby and Hippo.
"Hello," calls Alligator.
He runs up to them.
He does not see the flowers
by the path.

"Watch out," cries Hippo but it is too late. Alligator crushes all the flowers. "Oops," says Alligator. Baby Kangaroo starts to cry. Kangaroo picks him up and puts him into her pouch. "Come on, Hippo," says Kangaroo. "We shall go over the river." They cross the river on the stepping stones.

85

"Sorry, everyone," shouts
Alligator.
"Stay away from us," calls
Hippo.
Poor Alligator! He sits down
beside the crushed flowers.
He feels sad.
"Nobody likes me because
I spoil everything," he says.
"I wish my feet and tail were
not so big and clumsy."

The sun goes in and it gets very
cold. The wind begins to blow
and the raindrops start to fall.
It rains and it rains.
Soon the river is full.
Alligator can hardly see
the stepping stones at all.

He sees his friends on the
other side. He runs down
to the river.
"Help! We cannot get back!"
they all cry.
"I can help," says Alligator.
He steps into the river. He digs
two big feet into one bank,
and two big feet into the other.
"Jump on," he calls.

One by one, the animals step
onto Alligator's tail and walk
across his back to the other side
of the river.
"Three cheers for Alligator,"
says Kangaroo when all the
animals are safely across.
"We are very pleased to have
a friend with such big feet
and such a big tail."
Alligator smiles a very big smile.